I0621495

Immortalized in Ink

and other stories by

ARIA GLAZKI

ANIKA PRESS

FROM THE AUTHOR:

Soon after venturing into the online writing community, I was lucky enough to find Rebekah Postupak's Flash! Friday contest, complete with weekly story prompts and an enthusiastic group of writers. It was a wonderful way to flex my rusty writing muscles, and many of the stories in this collection first came to life as entries for that contest. Though they have since been revised, the stories included nevertheless reflect their roots, ranging significantly in style and genre. Some are heart-warming, some fantastical, and some quite dark. Several include dragons, stemming from Flash! Friday's completely reasonable obsession with the creatures, and possibly fueled a bit by my own love for them.

Whether you dive in and read the whole collection at once or use these stories as bite-sized reading breaks from a hectic life, I hope within these pages you'll find pieces that speak to you. And I'd love to hear your thoughts after you're done reading!

Before this note ends, I must take the opportunity to extend heartfelt gratitude—

to Rebekah: Without your contest and the welcoming community you fostered, most of these stories literally wouldn't exist.

and to Kristyn, Jennifer, and Brigid: Without your feedback, the resulting collection wouldn't have been half as readable.

CONTENTS

Immortalized in Ink

IMMORTALIZED IN INK

When was the last time you died?

They say the pages give you lives—open the cover and step through. Escape into the words and find your solace, or adventure. Everything you never knew you needed exists within a book.

Until the story ends.

I've lived a thousand lives, and none at all. Each time the cover opens, the path begins anew, an invitation to the reader to walk, hop, duck, devour, run—or linger. Meander through new minds.

How do you read?

Infuse the lines with life. You trade yourself for moments, thoughts that aren't yours yet wait for you—your heartbeats, gasps, and sighs the only way to matter. The pages flip at fingertips then flutter shut, marked, altered. Characters still, frozen and impatient.

Yearning.

Under your eager eyes they breathe again, huddled in armchairs or splayed out on the floor, cradled in your hands once more until that final page, your fingers' parting touch a bittersweet caress.

My story stops but doesn't end.

Shut on the shelf, I wait for you, your children, friends. I've memorized the words, the whole of my existence, unchanging. Emotions laid out in snapshots, catalogued yet incomplete, mold to their reader's temperament, rely on your vicissitudes.

Trapped in my life, I live it over with you.

You laugh, learn, ache, love, grieve, then shed my story like old skin, discard it on a growing pile. Husks wither, dry, decay, but pages stay, a fresh supply.

Immortalized in ink, I wait, and never die.

BARGAIN

Waking up isn't easy when you're being baked alive.

A groan scratches its way out of my throat as I open my eyes to the blistering sunlight. Soreness in my shoulders and ankles dissuades me from moving.

One of only two shadows on the sand moves. Grit scrapes my eyes as I try to blink the motion away.

"Oh shut up." The shadow falls over me for a blissful instant of relief, chased away by her grin. "How ya doin' down there?"

"What the hell you stupid—"

"Ah, ah. Careful."

The scorching spotlight finds my face again. She spits, taunting me with the waste of water.

"You owe me," I remind.

"Well now, that's why I'm here. You forget my little debt, and I'll cut you free."

"Are you off your—"

"Or." Her shadow moves out of sight. "I could just leave you here, while I come up with the money." A casual shrug shifts her shoulders. "Shouldn't take more than a couple weeks."

EXCEPTIONAL

Dozens of faces watch me take my place on the satin aisle spread along the sand. Waves lap quietly at its other edge. Heaping plates of food wait back at my parents' house.

The Council Head nods. I pop open my crimson umbrella and step forward.

When was the last time one drowned? a voice whispers.

Every Sinamee girl strides into the sea on her eighteenth birthday. An hour later, most reemerge—"purified." A handful never makes it back.

Every girl wears crimson, probably so we're easier to see out in the churning water. Every girl chooses her own accessory.

Neck-deep, I lower my umbrella over my head and push off, losing the bottom. The chant begins, marking my minutes in the water.

There's no time to scream when something grabs my leg, dragging me under. The umbrella's slick handle slips through my fingers as I kick out, thrashing to reach the fading light of the surface.

A band crushes my lungs as I give in.

But moments later my mouth gasps in air, and my eyes open to a shimmering hall, its walls encrusted with ancient crimson. Submerged beauty engulfs me as smiles greet my surprise. Faces we thought lost surround me.

Up on the surface, tonight's celebration will transform to distant vigil. But for the first time, I am home.

REGENESIS

The breeze plumps and shifts my hair, gently caressing the graying strands. The valley I live for stretches below, at last vibrantly verdant. A wash of life carpets the scars of war etched into the land.

My scars have found an uglier comfort, puckering and pulling at my skin. But inhaling the tangy bite of the surrounding vines soothes my once-rampant vanity.

My degenerating body served me well, fighting to carry me back to my one-time home and newfound haven, even if the bell tower is all that's left.

Once, this had been Castle Creagh.

Once, I'd been its queen.

Once, dragons had ruled the sky.

Now, amidst the ruins and foliage, only I remain, freed from the cage of bloodshed.

Ignoring my provisions, I watch the sun paint my land in its descent, allowing forgotten peace to droop my eyelids.

Until a flicker of fire reanimates my drained form. A second flicker reminds my lips of their former curve as my eyes search the horizon.

Yes—there. Wings.

We've made it home.

THE WAY BACK

Five more days.

Ashton had spent decades studying. When he'd finally finished his calculations, his heart had stilled with hope he'd barely dared to feel. He'd checked and checked again, and then he'd started gathering supplies.

Tired, blistered hands pulled the mound of silk he'd painstakingly stitched together closer. All he had to add were the ropes he'd woven. Then it would be time to climb.

His last jump taunted him. Floating over pristine peaks of snow, caressed by golden light... He saw it in his dreams, and in his nightmares. He'd been young and for those precious moments finally at peace, safely suspended by a sky-borne jellyfish over unparalleled beauty.

Until a force he'd given his life to understand had ripped him from that harmony.

Five more days until the anniversary of that interrupted jump, a hundred years from now and thirty years ago.

Five more days, and his only chance.

Ashton had to be ready.

FLIGHT PLAN

She could jump.

The darkened crevice yawned before her, trembling under the weight of her pursuers' pounding progress. In the distance, a carved bridge mocked her with its illusion of proffered safety. But she knew where it led.

At the very least, falling into the jagged void offered her an instant—of flight, of safety.

Of freedom.

An instant, before unforgiving stone tore her flesh, relishing the taste of blood that would feed the flecks of living greens. A gust of warmth blew over her, fluttering the tatters hanging from her frame.

Staring into the hungry depth, she could feel their relentless approach, inching closer to surround her, blocking any other chance of escape.

It was the crevice, or nothing. Worse than nothing—a future back in *his* hands.

His minions advanced slowly, certain she wouldn't risk plummeting to an inevitable death.

But she could jump.

And she just might survive.

IN LIVING COLOR

I trudge through the sludge, encased in browns and grays. Blindly, I shove my door open and continue toward the back, discarding pieces of my day—purse, gloves, coat, keys all dropping on any handy surface.

A crimson shadow shimmers, and I pause. A headshake clears my sight, stealing the hint of hope.

My eyes shut against the heartache, the memory of a world with color.

Hot breath on my face makes my heart stutter, my eyes snap open. Ash turns to embers, searing through veins that zing to life in a wash of lava. Purples and greens and golds all bloom in me anew.

Wing brushing wing, reunited we flew.

PERSPECTIVE

Jessie stepped back from the wall and winced. Her mural had started out innocently enough: a tree branching in seemingly unlimited directions. She'd woven a padlocked chain around the branches for the slightly heavy-handed metaphor of unlocking one's path in life. Boring.

The whole point was to inspire Brent's students, so she'd opened a window into another world, right there in the tree trunk. Then everything had spun out of control.

A board popped up in the center of the wall, standing at the edge of a cliff, with its own face and a snail handle. A flying carpet hovered over the chasm, carrying a unicorn and a fairy that accidentally resembled a prettier, glammed-up version of Jessie herself. The colors of the fairy's wings bled into her hair. Jessie'd added a dragon soaring far below for perspective. Plus, the unicorn liked watching them fly by.

She wiped her hands on her unsalvageable, paint-splattered pants and glanced at the clock ticking away over the blackboard. She slipped her brush through the yellow on her palette and resumed painting, driven to fill the empty patch on the left-hand side. Not that she had a deadline, per se. But the asymmetrical shapes blended with unexpectedly clean lines and spurred her on.

Soon a pensive, barefoot man filled a lone chair set at a table rooted to the ground. Chin in hand, he stared at the face on the not-quite-door that blocked him from the visitors suspended mid-air.

Jessie blinked then stared at the snail as it crept up the wooden panel. She shook her head. The unicorn beside her whinnied, and wind ruffled her wings.

Her wings?

Jessie searched for the clock, the blackboard, the alphabet border trim... Only mountains and sky surrounded her.

The man stood and approached the cliff's edge. He hesitated, chestnut eyes meeting Jessie's. A warm, calloused hand helped her step off the carpet rippling under her feet. He smiled, and Jessie's heart inexplicably lightened at the stranger's happiness.

It's official. Brent's going to kill me.

Heritage

Jackie stepped forward as the crowd thinned in the cavernous Louvre hall that housed *La Gioconda*. Throngs of tourists had filled virtually every inch of floor space for hours, jostling each other for a glimpse of the mysterious masterpiece that had sparked infernos of critical debates.

Now Jackie was the only one left, apart from Gioconda herself. Guards' footsteps echoed in the labyrinth of halls. Jackie steeled herself and squared off with the painting.

Masterful draping hid the dislocated shoulder which itself was covered by an intricate birthmark even the artist hadn't known was there. Jackie's hand brushed her own shoulder. Gioconda's eyes narrowed behind the thin barrier of the painting's protective glass.

Jackie stepped back involuntarily, her hand coming to rest just below her belly button. Her chin lifted a notch, and her eyes took in the soft curve of lips that had benefited from Da Vinci's love-struck generosity. She'd come here to make sure, but it was true: they were still safe.

Bewitching her ancestor had been called. If they only knew...

LOOKOUT

The tram screeched as it began its descent.
One.

It took thirty seconds to reach the bottom.
Two.

Luke shut his eyes.
Three.

He didn't have to watch it fly above the snowy valley.
Four.

Breathe.
Five... Six... Seven... Eight.

This tram was one of the fastest in the world.
Nine.

Twenty-three passengers.
Ten... Eleven... Twelve.

He forced his eyes open.
Thirteen.

His exhale steamed from his mouth.
Fourteen.

Luke pressed the button.
Fifteen.

Flames erupted in the ice-cold air.

DESERTED

There's something to be said for war. Nothing good, mind you. But something.

Landscapes lay littered with carcasses—human, wooden, metal… The war doesn't discriminate. But once abandoned, a war-torn carcass can transform into shelter, even nourishment, if you're desperate enough.

By the time I saw what used to be the Malika, I was desperate. When I made it inside its overturned husk, I thought I was saved. And I was, from the torture of a relentless sun and the stinging of windblown grains of sand. Even from the pursuit of army hard-asses. I slept for at least a day.

But my soul?

I try not to think about it.

I can still hear the war, at night, sometimes, but I'm too far for them to find me now. Escaped from the horror of man, now victim to the vicissitudes of the desert.

Metal bones and human ones offer me supplies as I balance my options. Stay inside and run through my scavenged resources, or venture out with the ones I can carry in a former soldier's bag?

It's not right, stealing from the fallen ones, salvaging their flesh for my survival.

But I was desperate.

SPEECHLESS

Herman hooked his cane on the wooden pew then knelt, bowing his head before the Virgin Mother whose gaze he hadn't met in years. The stone floor cushioned his knees, worn from his daily visits.

Fingers brushed his forehead, chest, and shoulders, and a sigh passed through his lips. Blankness filled his mind where prayer should have been. Would he ever find the words?

People cried in the streets, clinging to each other. A pale girl gasped, clutching her rounded stomach as rough hands knocked her down, disregarding the life within.

Every time he closed his eyes, such echoes of the past tormented him.

Skeletal bodies marching to their doom, torn from their homes and stuffed into stripes. Hopeless expressions on faces of all ages, cordoned off by barbed wire.

He'd done as he was told. Now he yearned for the forgiveness he didn't deserve.

Piles and piles of lifeless flesh.

And everywhere the yellow stars.

IN THE END

I freeze the moment I see him. Paint streaking his torso gives him away before my eyes even notice the ancient tribal artifacts cradled by his hands. I played with replicas when I was young, when New York was nothing more than a distant mystery, calling me away.

Skyscrapers, taxicabs, rude gestures, even the scents of the city I traded my soul for all fade into nothing as we lock eyes. His hair lies still, but mine whips around me in the eerie burst of air the moving bodies surrounding me don't notice.

A certainty I've never known before pours into my chest. One blink, and he would be gone.

One blink.

I know it, fear it, pray for it, though I doubt he would listen. My eyes water, then burn.

Gluskab gazes through me, into me, and not at me at all. Everything I've done, and he's still come. My knees hit pavement, sending up a spray of golden dust from home. My throat closes against the trite words that claw at my insides. A tear slips from my eye.

It hits the ground together with my head, and hands push through the haze, shaking me as people yell.

Forgive me.

But Gluskab turns away.

And my eyes fall shut.

Throwing children out of windows isn't normal. At the height of their trajectory, they float for a heartbeat in the air. Orange light paints over their skin. It's almost beautiful, but it isn't normal.

Some of the older kids understand, and they all fight our holds instinctively in fear. But we're stronger, and we're determined. Their wiggling and crying cannot slow us down. Screams tear through me, but I don't even pause.

"I hate heights," the little boy in my arms whispers.

"Close your eyes," I can't help whispering back.

The second he does, I clench my jaw and toss. His arms flail as he flies. *Fourteen.*

I pray the hands outside will catch him.

We search the smoky room for any small bodies left behind. The flames lick at my feet through the remaining patches of floor.

This isn't what I signed up for.

ON THE JOB

"Well? Where are my eggs?"

The boys shrink into the doorway, their white uniforms streaked with grime.

"Coon kem," Jordy mumbles, staring at the floor.

"What? Speak up!" My hands slap, pommel, and knead the dough for tonight's supper.

Jordy's eyes flick to his younger brother, then he squares his shoulders and notches up his chin. "We couldn't get 'em."

"And why not?"

The boys exchange glances. "We ain't big 'nough," Brady pipes up.

"Aren't," I snap, then sigh, setting the dough to rise. "Come on, I'll show you again." They're more than old enough to pull their weight.

Brady clutches Jordy's apron. The older boy has paled; his eyes have doubled in size.

"You can watch from outside," I relent, shaking my head. "Now go!" Seconds later, the boys reach their positions by the fence, peering through the slats. Seeing them, a couple more of the farmhands make their way over, feigning disinterest but throwing looks my way.

Iridescent wings flap as I enter the mammoth barn, and I pause until they still. It doesn't take long for my beauties to settle. I click my tongue three times, lifting my hand to pat the head closest to me, then untie the bag at my waist and move toward one of the piles of shining, delicate orbs.

Awed murmurs drift toward me as I collect my dragons' eggs.

Winter's Refuge

Shadowed figures plodded toward her, silhouetted against the setting sun. They blended together into one undefined mass, then separated into two distinct lumps—one half the size of the other—and congealed again, morphing with each movement.

Lacey let her book drift to her lap as she watched the slow progression through the steam around her cottage. The kitchen timer sounded, calling her away from the mesmerizing sight so that dinner wouldn't burn.

A steady crunching accompanied the sounds of lasagna being pulled out of the oven and set on the counter. They were getting closer. Lacey left the oven open so its heat flooded the small kitchen and adjacent living room.

The crunching grew louder then suddenly stopped. Lacey's head swiveled to watch the front door open to reveal two looming lumps. She dropped the oven mitts.

The smaller shape barreled toward her, shedding white powder all over the wooden floor.

"Mommy!"

BELOVED

When the climb leveled out, I thought we'd made it, but soon I saw all we have is more to go. The air is thin and crisp, pricking my lungs, but the stones are sun-warmed, and the smells of life surround me. Ahead is all that matters.

Almost all. Adam walks beside me, leaning on a dry, gnarled branch worn smooth from his handling. I know better than to touch it. I just keep going, keeping pace with him as we wind through the mountains. The stick supports his weight, but when his hand brushes me, I know. Even here, surrounded by the rawness of nature, he needs me at his side.

"You wanna take a break?" he asks, and he's already found the perfect place. We're alone out here, but we're together, and that's more than good enough. It's everything.

He drops his pack and sits, back braced against a slope padded with springy greens. I plop beside him. We share water from his bottle, and, satisfied, I lay with my head in his lap. His hand settles on me, fingers digging into my fur. There's nowhere I'd rather be.

TREASURE HUNT

It should have been beautiful. A hazy green cushions the uneven dusting of stars that coat the indigo sky. From where I stand, the brightest star hangs over the single shelter in sight, a beacon. The red of their light glows like an ember, reaching through the sky and sweeping over the snow.

Behind the light, flags mark space that would have otherwise looked endless. One dips to brush the powder, bending under the weight of its secrets.

They stand untouched by the light. I stand in the shadows.

It should have been beautiful, but I know what lays below, concealed by the snow and marked by vinyl triangles that chill my heart more than the temperature ever could.

"We'll be frozen in time," Jared whispered our last night together. "Promise you'll wait for me."

I promised, and we burned together in a night to remember, but then he left, for the opportunity of a lifetime.

Now the gleaming red exposes their furnace. It couldn't touch the heat of our love, but out in the cold, it burned him up. They dropped promises like breadcrumbs, then buried the lies. I don't bother counting the markers littering an expanse too sinister for its splendor. There's only one body that matters under this blanket of snow.

I promised to wait, but I know better than to waste both our lifetimes. They've stolen him from me.

And I have come to get him back.

QUARANTINE

Haze stings my eyes as I watch the village burn. Its wooden skeleton hisses and pops, collapsing under the flames. A wave of heat hits me as the steeple topples. Wails pierce the air.

I close my eyes, still seeing the families huddled under burning beams, corralled by fire.

The disease burns with them.

Victims of the virus hover above our home, bellowing. Shimmering scales shelter their once-human flesh from the ravenous flames. Once swallowed by sickness, they're invincible.

Cruelly magnificent wingspans fan their fire, a grasp at salvation for the infected but not entirely transformed. Schoolchildren, lovers, parents, friends—the disease didn't discriminate.

Only I stand immune, alone.

Heartbroken memories drip out of my eyes, evaporating instantly.

Impossibly elegant, one victim's heaving bulk lands beside me without a sound. A massive eye fills my vision, shining in the firelight. Tentative, I trace the new face of the man I love.

PASSING TIME

The ground pressed against him each time his lungs expanded. Clouds floated languidly above, framed by the perfect rectangle of the silent courtyard's buildings. Light glinted off a smattering of windowpanes. A single attic window broke the symmetry. A diagonal slant in one corner drew his attention next.

Jay closed his eyes. A graying replica of the walled-in expanse above him echoed in his mind. He focused on drawing in a clean breath from the copper-tinged air.

Memories of Maria's sensual lips and electrifying eyes replaced the innocent clouds. He could melt away into her smile.

Jay dug his fingers into the patchy grass below him and raised his eyelids. The picture had changed. The rest of his life could be spent watching new images, framed by the rooftops, appear between blinks.

He had to move.

Clenching his fists in the earth, he pressed his torso up. Starbursts colored the picture above him as the walls faded. This wasn't right. His shoulders dropped the few inches back to the ground, and blackness covered the sky.

Children's shouts forced his eyes open again. A small, dirt-smeared face appeared in the picture. A blink later it had vanished.

He couldn't stay there.

His hands flattened against the ground, ready to lift. Shaking muscles strained to raise his torso. His palm slipped in the stickiness that had seeped out of him as clouds danced in and out of his vision.

Jay slumped to the blood-coated ground.

Maria...

LEGACY

My spare key clatters into the bowl by the door, disturbing the quiet. I stop first by the record player I could have sworn Cal kept just for me, and switch on his last record. His voice, so filled with warmth, scratches through the emptiness of the living room.

Dim light fights its way through the windows, into the stillness, onto the dust. I sink onto the couch, motionless as memories surround me. He sings of our first touch, the pouring rain that prompted our first kiss. An eternity ago.

Wistfulness edges the lyrics. *We'll never have another first one*, he murmured when I mustered up the courage to ask why.

Soft footsteps pad across worn wooden floors, stopping by my feet. I reach out, scooping Cal's puppy into my lap. He whimpers, staring at me with shining chocolate eyes.

"I know, buddy," I whisper, curling my fingers into golden fur. "I'll miss him too."

WINTER PROMISE

Molly promised Tommy on his second birthday that every year they'd build a snowman. It wasn't an obligation she took lightly. Each year since, the miserable weather of December somehow gave way to a crisp, picturesque day, perfect for creating their masterpiece.

By Tommy's tenth, their favorite field was deserted, but the silence simply left more room to grow this year's temporary friend. Crunchy flakes of snow rolled easily into a lumpy base. By the time the torso had been clumped together and stacked, hints of icy moisture seeped through colorful gloves.

Feet were stamped and fingers flexed to restore blood flow before rolling the head. A stack of branches picked from a neighboring fence of pines was recruited to add reaching arms, verdant buttons, and brown eyes. Tufts of needles quickly transformed into hair. They always used the same pipe for a mouth.

Shivering, Molly stepped back to survey the snowman. It grinned back as grief squeezed her heart. "Happy birthday, Tommy," she whispered to the darkening sky.

Leigh never looked back anymore. She clenched her fingers around the loose elastic of his sweater and put one foot in front of the other.

The old bridge creaked a melody she'd memorized long ago. She made this walk at least once a week, sometimes more when there was exciting news to share. Like today.

She wore his sweater every time, but then, she wore it almost always, except when her mom convinced her otherwise. The elastic had lost its snap, drooping low over Leigh's hips, and the color had faded until it was nearly indiscernible. But it was still her favorite.

On the other side of the bridge, Leigh paused. Her fingers found the grooves etched into the wood years ago, worn smooth by the constant attention of her hands. He'd marked the bridge to outlast them both. It was their secret.

Leigh hiked the sleeves higher on her arms and brushed back her hair. He loved it long, so she'd never cut it.

She huddled in his sweater, caressing the crude heart that housed three sets of initials. The sun dipped into the river, reflecting off the water to color the foliage around her. Sometimes, she wished she could stay rather than turning right at the forked trail that led home.

She could make the trip in the dark, but her mom still worried. And they were celebrating tonight. For a heartbeat, Leigh considered turning back. She could sleep in the secluded grass, under a starlit sky untouched by the harsh world that waited. He would be close, and his sweater would keep her warm.

Forget that he would never walk her home.

Forget he couldn't hold her.

Forget he'd never know.

Leigh dropped to her knees, the college acceptance letter drifting to the ground. "I miss you, Daddy," she whispered to the wind.

ALL IN YOUR HEAD

I can still remember the last time. The clouds parted, the downpour paused, and light peeked through.

I don't think of the date. How much time has trickled past, swept along in the perpetual flood? Puddles ooze around my feet, pulling as I try to move away, to hide. No refuge in sight, they convince me to stay, to sink. Inch by miserable inch.

Soaked through, I've forgotten warmth, but there was a moment. The brush of sunlight seeped through the press of fabric, lightening the wet weight that drowns me. In its rays I caught a crisp breath, a lie refreshing my lungs.

An exhale later the rain resumed. It always does. A mist, a sprinkle, a drizzle, a shower growing into a deluge, sealing me in, rooting me to the spot.

Any spot, every spot. A step here or there, even if I could take it, would change nothing.

In the distance sometimes, a haze flickers beyond the water. As I blink away the drops clinging to my lashes, it disappears.

I've long learned to ignore the illusions, the deceptive glimmers of hope hovering beyond my reach.

But that happiness… It touched me, once.

UNTETHERED

On Friday, everything changed.

Every smile, every tear, every argument. Snapshots flipping past. None of them matter now. Yet nothing else does.

The chains of your love, the weight of expectations, the guilt of failure…

What am I, left without you? Who can I be if not yours—to mold, to want. To own.

Freed from you, I'm bound by memories, grasping as they slither through my fingers and out of my mind.

Dripping drops echo in the emptiness left behind.

Condolences whisper past, brushes of hands pressing mine with murmured prayers as sympathy arrangements bleed through the walls.

Dotted in crimson, I'm not free after all.

BE A MAN

You throw your dinner 'cross the kitchen, furious at its imperfect temperature. She cowers in the corner.

"A man is always in control."

Doors slam as you rampage through the house. She used to hide us in the cupboards, trembling.

"A man's home is his castle."

"Weak," you'd call me if I run to her side.

So I wait, until you tire of your attack. Wait, to catch her sobs in my embrace. And I hide—my drawings, my feelings, my self.

But your fists find their target, and I flinch. So a smack spins my head as you command, "Man up!"

Precise punches make for easily hidden bruises. Her stomach, her ribs, her thighs—anywhere clothing will cover. Because you're always in control.

The world outside will never see, but you demand I watch, and learn.

So I wait.

For the strength to fill my muscles and my heart. For the will to stand against your voice. For the courage to take your blows.

Fists hit flesh, blood blooms, but now I do not flinch. You taught me better.

She gasps, hand fluttering to her lips.

You stumble back—shocked. Out of control. Afraid.

But best of all away from her, from them, all huddling at my back. My fingers flex as I stand, a wall you can't take down. A shield to save them.

At last, a man.

INSTITUTION

Macey froze just inside the gate. Her legs refused to carry her any further. Her lungs couldn't find air to suck in. The symmetrical building stretched austere before her, framed by trees that should have been welcoming. She shut her eyes and swallowed.

More than a decade had passed since she had left the Holby Children's Home. The flaking paint of her past had nearly disappeared from its turrets.

Memories assaulted her mind, mirroring the years she'd spent inside. Hands she couldn't avoid brushing against her. Days spent in darkness, praying the insects in her hideaway weren't the kind that would bite. Being pinched, and prodded, and pulled to placate visitors in business suits. Investigators.

Conmen.

Her fingernails bit into her palms, surfacing her from the onslaught enough to draw in a single breath. Macey shrugged the memories away and forced her eyes open. Abandoned, the home should have looked worse than in her memories. An impossibly tall order.

The taxi still stood, less than ten steps behind her. They could turn around, drive away. She could leave this place to rot on the outside like it had long ago on the inside. As the one surviving resident, she had been offered the run of the land like some kind of twisted restitution.

Potential, they had said, over and over.

Hell, her mind had whispered.

Now the windows whispered it for her. She never should have come.

Hands dropped on her shoulders. Macey shuddered, but these weren't memories to be shrugged away. Soft circles brushed over stone muscles. Air flooded the space around her, and her lungs ached with renewed life.

Wind fluttered through the leaves. The hands fell away, but warm fingers soon tangled in hers, squeezing gently. Sunlight she hadn't been able to feel pierced through the misery. Trey had that effect.

Her gaze fell to an illuminated patch of lawn. A tiny blossom winked a fragile promise.

INSURGENT

The reflection set before me looks nothing like the girl I used to be. Even beneath the meticulously applied makeup, I wouldn't find her.

Costumers' hands primp and prod, tugging body parts out of the way and into place, wrapping me in strips of fabric, dotting me with gems. Hours and years spent preparing for tonight. Falsely elongated lashes skim my cheeks as the final piece is settled on my head, a feathery contraption concealing the precise styling below.

Silence whispers through the dressing room as all but my trusted attendant shuffle out. One more measured breath and then a timed introduction streams through the obscured speakers. Voices bounce around the hall outside, doors sporadically slapping shut as girls troop obediently to their designated platforms, ready for tonight's dignitary-studded audience.

I meet the orchid gaze that found then molded me, standing steadfast at my side until my acquisition by Seasoned and every moment since. Mask in place, Hitaré sprays me with a protective sheen then dusts me in the shimmering concoction of his creation, the poison indistinguishable from Seasoned's regulation glitter. An extra coating covers my décolletage, ready for the brush of official fingertips, the taste of entitled tongues.

A rap of knuckles calls me to the center post for the ultimate performance. My last—and theirs.

"No, see, the light's still not right," Danny said, taking in the scene set before him.

"Yeah, I got it. Fellas! Let's shift four over." The crew scurried to obey John's instructions.

Their star shook her head impatiently.

"If she keeps moving, we'll have to reset," Mason muttered.

"Try to stay still, Lill," Danny called.

Lilliana's tongue snaked out in a frustrated motion. Everyone but Danny backed up, unable to stifle the instinct. A low, deep laugh echoed out from Lilliana's glistening body, elegant in its unabashed girth. Her spectacular eyes narrowed on the trembling intern holding the nearest reflector.

Mason and John didn't notice, bickering as usual.

"Wait, look," Danny whispered, shutting them up. "If we just tilt the camera, the angles will be perfect! We'll get everything." He smiled and flicked the switch to record. Lilliana might be difficult, but she was also the key to his success.

As if proving his point, she spread her incandescent wings, eliciting gasps and even a few screams from the newbies. She moved with lightning speed, snatching the intern in one elegantly manicured claw. Her head swiveled to the camera. "Can we break for lunch?"

HIDE & SEEK

Kaira's giggle echoed around her. The others would never find her in here!

Her lilac glow lit the air, casting shadows as she stretched in the near darkness. There wasn't quite enough space for her wings to expand, but she could always just crawl out. The rough texture of the walls entertained her fingertips as she waited.

"Kaiiiiraaaaa!" Strum sang somewhere outside.

She pursed her lips and held her breath. Strum's hearing was the best of all of them, and sounds grew larger in here.

Thuds vibrated through her hiding place, and Kaira yelped, then sighed. Leave it to the humans to ruin their fun!

A shadow blocked the round entrance to her hideaway. "Gotcha!" Strum announced, standing on the iron lip.

Another thud knocked him off his perch, and he tumbled in, crashing into her. His fiery-golden glow joined hers, blending the colors against the perfect backdrop of the darkness. Both giggled at the beauty.

"Shh!" Kaira chastised. "They'll hear us!"

"The humans? They never hear anything!" He settled next to her, leaning back against the sloping walls. "Great hiding place! You think the others will find us?"

A fizzing filtered into the iron tube.

"What's that?" Kaira asked, scrambling toward the exit. She didn't hear Strum's answer.

And the humans didn't notice the colorful mist trailing their cannonball.

FINAL EXAM

Malvina sighed, closing her eyes in a desperate attempt for inspiration. Discarded globs glinted dully around her. She'd have to remember to recycle it all, but for now, she had bigger problems.

There were only a few hours left before the deadline, and absolutely nothing original or even remotely interesting had come from her brain, her hands, or any other part of her. Everyone already saw her as a joke. She couldn't fail again.

She puffed her breath out, reopening her eyes. Wisps of gold danced among her fingertips as she molded a delicate, spherical cage that spiraled out in waves. It darkened with her plummeting mood. Maybe she just wasn't cut out for Creation.

She spun the trinket in her hand. It clinked on the translucent surface before her. On a whim, Malvina ignited a spark in its center, brows drawing together at the wash of light.

Maybe this one *could* become a star.

LOOKING DOWN

Miserable little twits.

In my day, we could dance *and* smile. We knew the importance of pleasing the crowd, eliciting their cheers and chants, and cries. We were proud to be chosen, to be honored by the Council.

I used to run to practice in my little leotard—never a second late. When they doled out our immaculately white dresses with the poufy skirts, I listened to every word of their instructions. We never got those pretty bows for our heads, but we still knew to smile.

The parade down the streets was our beginning. All those years of classes, the dedication... We were the best, and that dance was our farewell to the humdrum life.

Nothing like this year's girls—undisciplined and unappreciative.

Our parents cried too, but we knew to smile, dancing as our city's only hope.

These wretches aren't fit to sacrifice.

At Any Cost

They left me.

Dozens of years of research brought my team *here*. The sound of the ocean, the sandy beaches and devastating cliff faces, the squawks of local avifauna… None of that matters.

They followed me, yes, but they couldn't see.

The Fibonacci sequence, Occam's razor, Knot theory—it's all about the numbers. *They* did it for credit, for research… For resumes, or a trip to the island.

Too blind to catch the clues and weave the truth together.

Vines bend to my fingers' will, and I etch my numbers into the sand, surrounded by the stench of flesh.

I'm always there—*almost* there. I'll find it.

The bodies don't matter.

They didn't believe.

RESTRAINT

A soft breeze drifted through the lone window, sending specks of sand dancing over the slopes time had painstakingly built in the abandoned shack. Sunlight streamed in, too, but Deruk used the shifting light only to mark time. All he could see out the window was more sand, anyway.

Countless precious granules had drifted out the open door in the perpendicular wall, out of his reach. At least today's wind had brought more sand than it had stolen. His legs ached with the waiting, and blood pounded through his head, even after all these years.

For decades he'd strained, fighting to reach the shackles suspending him by his ankles, but not all immortals were strong. So Deruk collected mounds from the sand and waited. For the mounds to rise, for the shifting solidity to cradle his body and relieve the searing pain in his muscles.

For a chance.

Being upright would be bliss enough, but once his hands could reach the metal…

He'd find her.

And then he'd make her pay.

Informed Consent

I didn't know.

They promise you adventure, excitement—a life among the stars. Worlds waiting to be discovered and freedom, from the pain of a mundane life, of mediocrity.

You'd think there would be years involved, of training. But you'd be wrong. You sign, and you leave, packaged like living cargo. To explore the unknown, and report back if you survive. Not to return—never to return.

They found me, and I signed, and their machines, they chose my fate.

We're less expensive than robots, and easier to instruct. Expendable.

They sent me to this tunnel, and now, with nothing left to do, I walk to its bright light, finding trinkets to report, seeking their promises around invisible corners.

They promise you a galaxy and send you to the sky. But as you fly, the stars are just the dotted line.

TO THE MOON AND BACK

My bags are packed. Frayed at the edges, the suitcases stacked easily on the porch we'll soon leave behind. Our home on *Hope Street*, or so you named it. Five years we lived here together, if the machines can be believed. Back then I didn't count the days, swept away in the novelty, the adventure. In our love.

The promises you whispered became the cobblestones beneath my feet as I walk the craggy surface of the moon. Stars and satellites shine in the endless sky. I search it every night, though night and day have meaning only in my mind, defined by the relentless ticking of the clock beside our stove.

Three hundred and eighty days I've marked off on a makeshift calendar. Three hundred and eighty nights that I've spent staring, praying, hating you, and hoping.

You told me twenty-four. Thirty at the most. *Less than a month. You'll hardly miss me!* You laughed as I hugged you close.

Three hundred and fifty days you owe me, as I wait for the ship you set off to find—our next adventure in another corner of the universe.

My bags are packed.

Turn the page for a look at Aria Glazki's
full-length romances:

Mending Heartstrings

Tasting Temptation

Mortal Musings

Available everywhere books are sold—
and your local library!

Mending Heartstrings

ARIA GLAZKI

Forging Forever, Book 1

Kane's a country singer who's tangled with too many deceitful women. He's learned his lesson: girls are for flirting and fun; emotions are for his music. But after spending a night with an earnest woman unlike any he's known, he can't force her out of his mind. So he goes in search of the woman he knows only as "Elle."

On her last night in Nashville, the staunchly pragmatic Sabella found herself in a situation more suited to a romance novel than reality. Swept away, she ignored her rigidly self-imposed rules, succumbing to the fantasy just this once. But she knows real-world relationships have nothing in common with their fictionalized portrayals. When Kane unexpectedly shows up at her Portland apartment, she must choose between the practical truths she has learned and the desire for a passionate love she has struggled to suppress.

Despite the distance, Kane's tour schedule, and their meddling friends, both are drawn to the chance for a romance neither quite believes is possible.

Tasting Temptation

ARIA GLAZKI

Forging Forever, Book 2

After last summer's failed attempt at romance, Gina is absolutely done with men. And especially with millionaires. She has a good job as a fashion editor and amazing friends, and she's decided she needs nothing else. All she really misses is the sex. But that rush just isn't worth the risk of being ensnared in another relationship. When the hot bartender at her best friend's Sonoma wedding suggests some harmless stress relief, she takes him up on the offer. When it's sufficiently satisfactory, she indulges in a repeat—for the road. When she learns he's actually the wealthy owner of the vineyard, the mix of fury and fear is damped only by the knowledge that she never has to see him again.

Hunter Cavaliere is determined to honor his grandfather's legacy, and so far, he's right on track. The vineyard is thriving, he has plans for expansion, and his wines speak for themselves. The only thing missing is the right woman to share it all. But through his grandparents' marriage, Hunter learned what true love is, and he's unwilling to settle for anything else. A woman who judges him because of his money definitely isn't high up on his list. Still, when circumstance unbelievably keeps bumping him into the intriguing brunette from Portland, he can't shake the feeling that she is someone he should pursue.

Gina's poised to run the other way, but one more taste of Hunter may just prove too tempting to resist.

Mortal Musings

ARIA GLAZKI

Muse Alexandra has had it with the arrogant, ungrateful humans she is obligated to inspire. When the internal ranting of her latest charge pushes her past reason, she disregards the rules and forces her own words through his fingers, and is instantly entrapped in mortal form. With no magic, no identity, and no resources, Allie has no alternative but to navigate the mortal realm, depending entirely on her reluctant host while discerning what exactly caused her transformation—and how to reverse it.

Brett doesn't have a chance to consider the words that mysteriously showed up on his screen; he's too distracted by the stunning woman who appeared in his office out of nowhere. Before his brain can catch up, Brett's uninvited guest becomes enmeshed in his everyday life. Her artless innocence gradually lessens his suspicions. Most importantly, the writer's block that's been plaguing him dissolves under the fantasies the naively beguiling Alexandra inspires.

All too soon, the forced proximity sparks a confounding awareness neither writer nor muse are able to resist.

— ABOUT ARIA —

Aria Glazki's first kiss technically came from a bear cub. Though no fairytale transformation followed, she still believes magic can happen when the right people come together—if they don't get in their own way, that is. So now Aria writes heartfelt romances about relatable people overcoming real-world obstacles to build love that lasts.

Connect with Aria Online:

www.AriaGlazki.com

Newsletter: bit.ly/AriaGNewsletter

Facebook.com/AriaGlazki

Twitter & Instagram: @AriaGlazki